FASHION
ACADEMY

Model
Madness

FASHION
ACADEMY

Model
Madness

Sheryl Berk and Carrie Berk

sourcebooks
jabberwocky

Published by Sourcebooks Jabberwocky, an imprint of Sourcebooks, Inc.
P.O. Box 4410, Naperville, Illinois 60567-4410
(630) 961-3900
Fax: (630) 961-2168
www.sourcebooks.com

Library of Congress Cataloging-in-Publication data is on file with the publisher.

Source of Production: Versa Press, East Peoria, Illinois, USA
Date of Production: November 2016
Run Number: 5007873

Printed and bound in the United States of America.
VP 10 9 8 7 6 5 4 3 2 1

To Gaga: we love you oodles and always.

Fashion Fairy Tales

Mickey Williams flipped through the May issue of *Vogue*, mesmerized. How could every single page be so incredibly breathtaking? Gowns and jackets and ankle boots…oh my! She loved the feel of turning each glossy page and the smell of the perfume ads. She unfolded one called "Destiny" and inhaled deeply. It smelled like fresh roses with a hint of vanilla.

Her aunt Olive was seated next to her on

the couch and wrinkled her nose. "What is that smell?" She looked up from her *New York Times* crossword puzzle and sniffed the air.

"Destiny," Mickey sighed.

"Smells more like my granny's attic," Olive insisted. "That powdery-sweet smell—mixed with mothballs."

Mickey rubbed the flap on her wrists. "I like it. It reminds me of Wanamaker's department store where Mom works." She looked at the time on her phone: 9:53 a.m. Her mother, Jordana, would be there right now, prepping the makeup counter, cleaning her brushes, and aligning her powders and shadows for the ten o'clock store opening. Her mom worked harder than anyone Mickey knew—seven days a week—and she understood why: "So my Mickey Mouse can have everything she needs to be a famous fashion designer one day."

Mickey could hear her mom's voice in her head, reminding her how important it was for her to do well at the Fashion Academy of Brooklyn, a.k.a. FAB. Jordana hadn't been all that eager to let Mickey leave her home in Philly to live with Olive in New York City. But in Mickey's mind, the decision had already been made. There was no other place she wanted to be.

Up until then, no one in her elementary school had really "gotten" her. They made fun of her handmade clothes and how she loved to stripe her hair with colored chalk and mismatch prints and patterns. Her out-of-the-box design aesthetic had secured her a full scholarship to FAB—and there was no way she was going to turn it down.

"Mom, please, pretty please with sequins on top?" Mickey had begged her.

At first, her mother had stubbornly refused. The city was a big, scary place, and Olive, her twin sister, had no experience raising a kid. But in the end, Mickey had convinced her mom that she would follow her aunt's rules, study hard, and make her proud—plus come home for holidays and as many weekends as possible.

"Fine." Jordana had relented. "I guess I can't stand in the way of your dreams."

That conversation seemed like ages ago, but it had been less than a year since Mickey had started at her new middle school. She'd made friends and frenemies, challenged herself with all kinds of crazy design projects, and even gone to Paris to compete against fellow student designers from around the world.

FAB was everything she'd imagined it would be and more—but on days like this, she missed her mom's chocolate-chip pancakes for breakfast and how the two of them would snuggle in bed and read the Style section of the Sunday

New York Times together. She missed the way they had always been a team, sharing their lives and their secrets.

Olive was great, and she could whip up an awesome tofu scramble for breakfast. But Mickey's mom was the one person—the only person—who knew her soul. Mickey remembered how, when she was five years old, Jordana would bring her home tiny vials of perfume samples from Wanamaker's. She pretended they were magic potions—one for love, one for beauty, one for wisdom.

"And this," her mom announced, "is a wizard's potion that grants you a magical wish!"

Mickey had clapped her hands together with glee. "Put it on me!" Her mom obeyed, dabbing a tiny bit of the scent behind Mickey's ear.

"And what do you wish for?" she asked.

The answer was easy: "Can we read *Vogue*?" Mickey pleaded.

Together, they would scan the pages, pausing every so often to ooh and aah over an outfit or accessory. Most little girls requested fairy tales for bedtime stories. But not Mickey.

"More, Mommy, more!" she pleaded. "Read me more about the fall collections."

At times, Jordana could barely keep her eyes open. She had waited on customers for eight hours, then had to tidy up the mess they left behind: product testers, cotton balls, and swabs.

"Mom." Mickey poked her if she started to dose off. "Read it to me. Again!"

"'Channel your inner animal with these jungle-inspired prints for fall.'" Her mom tried to stifle a yawn as she repeated the headline.

"Does that say *leopard*?" Mickey asked, pointing to a word on the page. She was barely in kindergarten, but she could already figure out most of what the articles said.

Her mother perched her reading glasses on the tip of her nose. "It says it's a jaguar-print midi dress by Givenchy." She read the caption on the photo carefully.

"Oh! Not leopard, jaguar," Mickey repeated after her. "It's beautiful."

"That it is," her mom said, planting a kiss on Mickey's forehead. "And it's also late and past your bedtime, Mackenzie Williams."

"Aw, Mom!" Mickey whined. "Just one more page? The one with the Versace zebra scarf on it?"

Jordana flipped to the next page. "Seriously, Mickey Mouse? You've memorized the entire issue already? It came two days ago!"

Mickey shrugged. The rest of her classmates

were just learning their ABC's and reading Dr. Seuss. "I can't help it. It's just so good!"

Olive waved a newspaper section in Mickey's face. "You want this?" she asked, giving the cover of the Style section a quick glance. "Something about a girl named Gigi looking pretty in pink."

Mickey grabbed the paper from her aunt and shook away the old memories. "Oh, it's Gigi Harlowe, the supermodel," she said. "She has such personal style!"

She held up the cover and showed her aunt a photo of the young woman dressed in a hot-pink strapless gingham dress, mile-high stiletto heels, and a wide-brimmed straw hat. She was carrying a Swarovski crystal–encrusted purse in the shape of a pig.

"What's with the little piggy purse?" Olive chuckled. "'This little piggy went to market. This little piggy stayed home…'"

"It's fabulous—bold, whimsical, one of a kind," Mickey insisted. "Everyone is going to want one. It's the new It bag."

"What's an It bag?" Olive asked.

"It's my Apparel Arts homework assignment,"

Mickey said, sighing. "Mr. Kaye insists we come up with a new It bag design for spring."

Olive shook her head. "I don't get *it*."

Mickey flipped to a photo in *Vogue* of Gigi strutting around SoHo with a royal-blue leather bag on her arm.

"See this? It's called the Sac de Jour by YSL." Mickey showed her aunt. "I have to come up with something equally 'impactful, innovative, and awe inspiring,'" she explained, quoting her teacher's instructions. Mickey knew that Mr. Kaye meant business. Anyone failing to wow him with their homework sketch might also wind up failing his Apparel Arts class for the semester.

"Not an easy task," Olive replied. "That's even harder than nine down: a five-letter word for trend ending with an *e*."

Mickey shrugged. "Craze?"

"Yes! That's it!" Olive cheered. "You're good at crosswords, Mackenzie!"

"Not really." Mickey blushed. "I'm good at fashion—but this assignment really has me stumped."

Olive put down her newspaper. "What can I do to help?"

Mickey sighed. "Unless you have a whole collection of vintage It bags hiding in your closet to inspire me, I don't think you can."

"Well, I have a whole collection of reusable bags for carrying my organic groceries," Olive offered. "They're in the cabinet under the sink."

"Thanks, Aunt Olive," Mickey said politely, "but Mr. Kaye is expecting a little more than a shopping bag. I have to come up with something *It*...or else."

2

School Daze

The next morning, Mickey dragged her feet into first-period Apparel Arts. She didn't feel like herself at all—even the outfit she'd put together felt uninspired. She'd chosen a simple pink tee, a jean vest, and navy leggings, and hadn't even bothered to mismatch her pink combat boots. It was so unlike her! The rest of her classmates were eager to show Mr. Kaye their ideas for the new spring It bag. But she wasn't feeling so enthusiastic.

"My purse is so cool," Mars said as Mickey took the seat next to her. Mars—like her name suggested—was a bit out there, but she was a brilliant jewelry designer. No one was as talented at working with gemstones and metals.

"Wanna see?" she asked Mickey, whipping open her sketchbook. "I call it the Iron Woman. See? It's a hobo constructed from woven chain links."

"Nice try." South, another of their classmates, pushed between them and pulled out her drawing. "I'm making a backpack with a built-in speaker so I can always play my tunes. Mine rocks...literally."

Mickey saw Mars's face fall. "Yours is good

too," Mickey whispered, trying to be complimentary. "It's very knight in shining armor."

Mars looked annoyed. "No, it's not. That's not what I was going for at all."

"Oh." Mickey tried to apologize. "I'm sorry. It's how I saw it."

"Well, you saw it wrong," Mars said, snatching her sketchbook away.

"Take it easy, Mars," Gabriel insisted. "Fashion is always open to personal interpretation. What does Mr. Kaye say? 'Every I has an eye'?" After repeating Apparel Arts for the second year in the row, Gabriel could quote all of Mr. Kaye's lectures. But he had a tough time applying those principles to his work. Somehow, things got lost in translation.

"So what did you sketch?" Mars asked him.

"Glad you asked!" Gabriel replied. He opened his book to a drawing of a graphic tote bag. On one side was a large letter *I* in white leather on a black suede background. On the other side was a large letter *T*.

"Get it? It's an *It* bag," he said, chuckling. "I know it's literal, but it's also really funny."

Mars smirked. "I hope Mr. Kaye has a sense of humor."

Gabriel's face went white. "OMG, he doesn't, does he?" He tore the page out of his pad. "I better start over!"

Jade Lee strolled into the classroom with her twin brother, Jake, trailing behind her. Mickey couldn't help but notice the tiara-like rhinestone headband Jade had chosen for herself this morning. In FAB, Jade was clearly the queen bee, but only because her mother was Hollywood fashion royalty—the designer most stars wanted to wear on the red carpet.

Jade loved to brag about rubbing elbows with celebs. Her Instagram was filled with photos of her with Kylie Jenner, Justin Bieber, and Selena Gomez. But despite all her bravado, Jade felt threatened by Mickey. Time and time again she tried to prove she was the better designer—which meant putting Mickey down and trying her best to sabotage her work.

"This assignment was so easy," Jade boasted to her classmates. "I mean, I own every It bag in existence. I'm an expert."

"So what did you design?" Mars asked her anxiously. "And remember, Mr. Kaye said you can't go over twenty dollars on materials."

"Duh!" Jade replied. "I don't need to. I'm planning on recycling."

"She means she plans on using some of the luxe fabric her mom has at her factory," Gabriel whispered to Mickey. "So not fair!"

Jade pulled out a sketch of a honeycomb-quilted

gold bag studded with tiny gold rivets. "I call it the Queen Bee."

Mars laughed out loud. "Well, that's predictable."

"It is not," Jade fired back. "It's entirely original. I've never seen anything like it."

Mickey hated to agree with Jade, but she was right. She'd never seen anything like it in all her years of reading *Vogue* and the Style section.

She glanced at the clock—it was 9:05. Where was Mr. Kaye? It wasn't like him to be late.

"So while we're waiting for our tardy teacher"—Jade read her mind—"what did you draw, Mickey?"

Mickey sank a little lower in her seat. "Me? I'd prefer not to share."

"Why?" Jade asked, raising an eyebrow. "We've all shown each other our designs."

Jake's hand shot up. "Not me. I haven't."

"Oh, who cares?" Jade barked at her brother.

"I do," Mickey replied, trying to shift the attention off herself. "Let's see what ya got, Jake."

Jake smiled and proudly displayed his sketch. It was a silver crescent-shaped bag. He held up a swatch of crinkly metallic fabric. "It's vegan leather," he explained. "It's my (Wo)Man in the Moon bag—and I think either a guy or a girl could carry it."

Jade rolled her eyes. "Where? To the gym? That's so not high fashion. Fake leather?

Pullease!" She turned back to Mickey. "Now it's your turn."

Before Mickey could protest again, Mr. Kaye dashed into the studio. "Dreadful traffic. Impossible!" he muttered under his breath. "A photo shoot with some supermodel was blocking the Brooklyn Bridge."

"Supermodel?" Gabriel's eyes lit up. "What supermodel? And is she still there? 'Cause I could go check for you…"

"Cece or Mimi or Fifi." Mr. Kaye tried to recall. "I follow fashion—not the models who wear it."

"Gigi?" South piped up. "Gigi Harlowe?"

"Yes, yes," Mr. Kaye said dismissively. "Gigi. That was her name. They closed the entire bridge for her. I had to actually get out of my cab and walk!"

"Not to worry." Jade smiled sweetly. "We were all discussing our homework assignments. Mickey wants to show you hers first."

Mickey gulped. Jade was relentless!

"Fine," Mr. Kaye said, taking a seat on the corner of his desk and mopping his brow with a hankie. "Mickey, please present your design."

Mickey opened her sketchbook to a blank page. "Um, I didn't get that far..." she began.

Mr. Kaye's eyes grew wide. "You didn't get

anywhere! Mackenzie, I'm shocked and disappointed." He took out his grading sheet. "That's an incomplete on your homework."

"I'm sorry!" Mickey tried her best to explain. "I spent all weekend on it, but I had designer's block. I couldn't come up with anything that felt right."

Mr. Kaye held up his hand. "No excuses. A designer must learn to break the block and tap into her own originality and creativity."

For the rest of the class, Mickey barely heard a word Mr. Kaye or any of the students said. She was too mortified: an incomplete! What would she tell her mom? When the bell rang, she wandered down the hallway and didn't even notice her best friend, JC, standing at her locker waiting for her.

"Helloooo?" he said, snapping his fingers to get her attention. "Earth to Mickey! Anyone home?"

"I got my first incomplete in Kaye's class," Mickey blurted out. "A big, fat incomplete!"

"Ouch," JC replied. The Chihuahua hidden in his bag barked in agreement. "Madonna seconds that. She says, 'That's ruff!' Get it? Rough?"

Mickey wasn't amused. "It isn't funny, JC."

"Sorry—a little doggie humor. How did you get an incomplete?"

"I didn't do my homework," Mickey said.

"Well, that'll do it! Why? You're so on the ball, Mick. It's not like you to blow off a Kaye assignment. It makes him see red!"

"I know!" Mickey exclaimed. "I didn't do it on purpose. I'm just blocked. I can't think of a single thing!"

JC nodded. "I see. You've caught designeritis."

"What?" Mickey gasped. "Is it serious?"

"Very," JC said, trying his best to keep a straight face as he teased his friend. "It comes on all of a sudden, without any warning, and can last several days without proper treatment."

"Oh no! Is there a cure? What should I do? Should I see a doctor?"

JC nodded. "Meet me after school, and I'll take you to a specialist."

Mickey nodded. "Okay—if you're sure it'll work."

JC smiled mischievously. "Have I ever led you wrong?"

3

The Doctor Is In

JC guided Mickey down a long alleyway in the East Village to a small storefront with no sign or awning. Black shades covered the windows.

"What is this place?" Mickey asked nervously. "Is it safe? It looks a little sketchy…"

"Of course it's safe, silly," JC said, ringing the front bell. "Madge is a good friend and an expert when it comes to designeritis."

"Madge? Who's Madge?" Mickey said.

A woman dressed in an eighties-style hot-pink jumpsuit with huge padded shoulders opened the door. *Well, at least she doesn't look dangerous,* Mickey thought. *Just a little retro…*

"That's my name—don't wear it out!" the woman said, ushering them inside. Her platinum-blond hair was tied in a huge, pink lace bow on top of her head, and she had stacks of rubber bracelets on both arms. Mickey noticed that this was no doctor's office. In fact, it looked like an eighties memorabilia store. Hanging from the ceiling were several disco balls, and on the walls were old record album covers and posters of eighties pop stars. An autographed Pat Benatar picture hung over the cash register.

"I don't get it. How is this gonna help?" Mickey asked, confused.

"Give it a chance, Mick. It always works for me," JC assured her.

Madge cleared her throat. "Don't be rude, JC. Introduce me to your friend."

"Madge, Mickey...Mickey, Madge," JC said.

Mickey smiled shyly. "Hiya."

"I like your pink highlights," Madge said, noticing Mickey's hair. "And the pink combat boots—nice touch."

"Mickey's one of a kind," JC said proudly. "But right now, we have a grave situation. She has an extreme case of designeritis."

"You don't say," Madge said, looking concerned. "That bad, eh?"

"The worst I've ever seen," JC replied.

Madge disappeared into the back of the store and returned with a huge carton of what looked like old records. "Debbie Gibson? Tiffany? Joan Jett? No, wait! Annie Lennox!"

JC shook his head. "I said this is serious."

Madge blew a huge pink bubble with the gum she was chewing. "I hear ya. Step back…"

She placed a record on an old turntable and gently rested the needle on the vinyl disc. "Dress You Up" began blasting.

"Early Madonna—good for whatever ails you!"

Madge said and started singing along to the tune with JC.

Mickey rolled her eyes. "JC, this is ridiculous. How is this going to cure my designeritis?"

"Let yourself go," Madge advised her. "Feel the music and let it inspire you!"

JC grabbed Mickey and gave her a spin. "Come on, Mick. Have you forgotten that fashion is supposed to be fun? Exciting? Uplifting?"

"I'm sorry," Mickey said. "It's just not doing it for me."

"Then try this," Madge said, pulling another disc out of her carton. "This one never fails."

As soon as the song started playing, JC's face

lit up. "My fave! 'Causing a Commotion' from Madonna's classic movie *Who's That Girl*. Crank it up, Madge!"

"Just let it fill your heart," Madge said, taking Mickey by the hands. "Doesn't the music make you feel happy?"

Mickey squeezed her eyes closed and tried to focus on the beat. "Um, no, not really. I just keep thinking of that incomplete on my homework."

JC sighed when the song ended. "Mickey, you're not trying." He held out his hand for Madge to give him a piece of bubble gum. "Seriously, I think you're contagious. You're making me feel sad and uninspired now."

"Tutti-frutti, Berry Bubble, or Watermelon Blast?" Madge asked, producing a fishbowl filled with wrapped pieces of gum that she kept beneath the counter.

"Lemme see that," Mickey said suddenly, grabbing the bowl away from JC.

"Gee, if you want a piece of gum, just say so." JC sniffed. "Pushy, pushy."

"This…" Mickey began. "This is it."

JC and Madge looked at each other, puzzled.

"Ya lost me there, Mick," JC said. "What's it?"

"Bubble gum," Mickey exclaimed. "I'm cured!"

Pop Star

Bright and early before Tuesday's classes started, Mickey knocked gently on Mr. Kaye's office door.

"Mackenzie, come in," he said. "I was expecting you."

"You were?" Mickey asked. "But how? I didn't make an appointment."

"I knew it wouldn't take you long to break your designer block if you put your mind to it. What have you got for me?"

Mickey pulled her sketchbook out of her back-pack. "I was thinking I could create a vinyl bag with a pink plastic window in the center."

"And the shape?" Mr. Kaye asked.

"Round—like a bubble," Mickey said confidently. "With a shoulder strap made out of gum wrappers woven together that can also double as a belt so you can wear it on your hip. I'd reinforce the strap, of course, with plastic."

Mr. Kaye studied the sketch without saying another word. Mickey held her breath and crossed her fingers.

"Good," he said finally. "Carry on."

Mickey smiled. "Really? It's okay?"

"It's better than okay. I said it was good," her teacher repeated. "Don't make me change my mind about erasing that incomplete."

Mickey skipped down the hallway and found JC in his usual spot waiting for her.

"Well?" he asked her anxiously. "Did he like it?"

"Yup," she said, beaming. "He said, 'Carry on.'"

JC handed her a pack of gum. "Then you better start chewing. I told Madge to save you all her gum wrappers too. Between the three of us, you'll have your It bag materials in no time."

"I think I'm going to call my bag the Pop Star," Mickey said. "What do you think?"

"I think the old Mickey is back," JC said, noting her paisley-print blouse and yellow plaid skirt. "And hopefully here to stay."

The week Mickey had to complete the project flew by, and this time, she couldn't wait to reveal her work to her class. She was so proud of how it turned out that she wore it to school that day—with a matching dip-dyed pink denim jacket she'd made as well, and pink high-top sneakers. She was waiting for the school bus on the corner of Columbus Avenue near Olive's apartment when a young woman in a ponytail and sunglasses jogged by. She suddenly stopped in her tracks, turned around, and stared at Mickey.

"Excuse me," she said. "That bag you're wearing? Where did you get it?"

Mickey's mom had warned her about talking to strangers, so she simply smiled and said nothing.

"Oh! You're afraid to talk to a stranger!" The woman smiled. "I'm not a crazy person, honestly! It's just that bag… It's amazing. I want it!"

Mickey clutched her purse tightly. "Help! Someone help me!" she started shouting and reached for her phone to call 911, just as her mom had instructed her. A man walking his dog came to her aid. "Everything okay, miss?" The dog snarled at the woman.

"No! She's trying to steal my bag," Mickey said. "I'm calling the police."

"Wait!" the woman said, pulling off her glasses. "I'm not a mugger. I'm a model!"

Mickey's mouth practically hit the pavement. "You're Gigi! You're Gigi Harlowe! The supermodel!"

"Oh! Can I have your autograph?" the man asked, handing her a napkin from his pocket for her to sign.

Gigi pulled a pen out of her fanny pack. "Yeah, sure." The man took a selfie, then continued on his way. But Mickey was too excited to stop gushing. "No one at FAB is going to believe this! Gigi and me...me and Gigi...on the same street!"

"Sh!" Gigi pleaded with her. "Please keep it down. I just gave the paparazzi the slip in the park."

"I can't believe it's you! I'm talking to you! I saw you on the cover of this month's *Vogue*—oh, and in the Style section."

"Can you tell me where you bought that bag?" Gigi pressed her. "I really need it."

"I didn't buy it," Mickey explained. "I made it."

"You made it?" It was now Gigi's turn to be shocked. "What do you mean? Are you a fashion designer?"

"Yes! Well, kind of. I'm a fashion designer in training. At the Fashion Academy of Brooklyn."

Gigi grabbed Mickey by the arm. "You have to let me buy it. It's divine. And you're sure no one else has one?"

Mickey shook her head. "Cross my stitches," she said. "It's one of a kind. I call it the Pop Star."

"I must have it." Gigi continued eyeing the bag from every angle. "I'm going to a Pink Party benefit at the Madison Plaza Hotel tonight."

Mickey was ready to hand over her purse and let Gigi model it at the posh fund-raiser until she remembered her assignment was due today. She couldn't risk another incomplete from Mr. Kaye.

"I can't," she said sadly. "My teacher will kill me. I have to present it to my Apparel Arts class this morning."

"Okay, okay." Gigi gave in. "But you can get it to me after school, right?"

Mickey nodded.

"Let me give you my cell, and you can text me when you're done with it. I'll get you the address of where I'll be," Gigi insisted.

"Your cell phone? You're giving me your phone number? So I can text you?" Mickey felt dizzy with joy.

"Yes. How else will you get it to me on time? Gimme your phone." She quickly typed her number into Mickey's contacts. "So send me a text later today and let me know what time. I'll figure out where we can meet up—I've got a crazy day of shooting around the city."

Mickey was trying to process what Gigi was saying. It sounded too good to be true. As if it wasn't all wonderful enough, Gigi added, "I'll pay you three hundred dollars. Does that sound reasonable?"

"Three hundred dollars? You're paying me three hundred dollars?" This time, Mickey couldn't keep her voice down. No one had ever paid her for one of her designs—much less a world-famous supermodel with 15 million followers on Instagram! She wanted to sing it from the city rooftops!

Gigi sighed. "Okay, five hundred dollars—but that's my final offer."

Mickey had to pinch herself to make sure this wasn't all a dream.

"Are we cool?" Gigi asked, checking her watch. "I gotta finish my run and get to the shoot."

"Cool," Mickey answered, still dazed.

"Awesome!" Gigi waved and jogged off just as the FAB school bus pulled up. The bus driver honked his horn. "Mickey, are you getting on or just standing there?" She felt like she was in a trance as she took a seat in the back of the bus. She

checked her phone, and there it was in her contacts: Gigi Harlowe. She typed a quick message—
Great meeting u!—to see if it was real or if Gigi
had just been pulling her leg.

Her phone dinged, and she read the response:
Great meeting u 2—c u later!

5

Gigi's Bestie

"You won't believe it!" Mickey said when she finally found JC waiting outside his History of Buttons and Bows class. He was trying to juggle his backpack, a huge garment bag, and Madonna's pink quilted doggie carrier when Mickey raced over and started shaking him.

"Easy! Easy! Dog on board!" he reminded her. "Madonna's got a sensitive tummy, and she's very susceptible to motion sickness…"

"You will never believe what happened this morning. Not in a million years. Try to guess," Mickey dared him.

"Let's see... You won the lottery? Madonna offered you a job as one of her backup dancers?"

"Better!" Mickey said, pumping his arm once again. "JC, I think I've died and gone to fashion heaven!"

JC raised an eyebrow. "Really? What happened?"

"Gigi Harlowe wants to wear my bag!" Mickey twirled around and showed him her finished bubble purse dangling off her shoulder. "She said she has to have it!"

"Nuh-uh!" he gasped. Now it was his turn to

jump up and down—despite poor Madonna's whimpers. "What? How? When? Where?"

"It all happened so fast," Mickey tried to explain.

"Every detail. Start at the beginning," JC insisted. "Don't leave anything out."

Just then the first-period bell rang. "Sorry, JC. I can't be late for Mr. Kaye's class," Mickey said. "I'll tell you later. At lunch."

"What? You can't leave me hanging like this!"

Mickey hurried down the hall but called out behind her, "Don't worry. We're hanging with Gigi after school today!"

All through the Apparel Arts presentations, Mickey couldn't help but smile and giggle to herself. She barely paid attention to any of her classmates' presentations or Mr. Kaye's critiques. All she could think about was what had happed this morning. What if a photo of Gigi wearing her purse made this week's Style section in the Sunday *New York Times*? What if every celeb in New York wanted to own the Pop Star purse?

"Mackenzie?" Mr. Kaye asked, noticing how distracted she seemed. "You've been very quiet. I hope that doesn't mean you have nothing to show us…again."

"Oh, I do!" Mickey said proudly. She went to

the front of the class and held her bag in the air. "I call it the Pop Star," she explained. "Get it? Like the pop of bubble gum, but also an eighties pop-star vibe?"

Mr. Kaye was silent. He walked around Mickey, examining the bag from every angle. "I was pleased with your concept for the design," he finally said. "But this final work falls short. The stitches are sloppy, and the shape is slightly more oval than round on one side, which indicates a flaw in the measurements. While it reflects a sense of creativity and whimsy, I'm sorry to say it's not your best work."

Mickey couldn't believe her ears. "Are you

kidding me? This bag is amazing. Gigi Harlowe wants to wear it to a huge, fancy fund-raiser. She thought it was the most incredible bag she'd ever seen, and she's paying me five hundred dollars for it!" She took a deep breath and blurted out, "What do you know anyway?"

The entire class gasped in unison. "She did not just say that," South whispered.

"He's going to blow his top!" Mars chimed in.

"Tell me when it's over," Gabriel said, covering his eyes.

"Miss Williams," Mr. Kaye fumed. His face was bright red. "For your information, I happen to know a great deal. I know that this bag shows a lack of finish and flair. I know your technique leaves a great deal to be desired. And I know what separates a good designer from a great one...modesty!"

"Wait." Jade interrupted Mr. Kaye's scolding. "Did she just say Gigi is wearing her bag to a fund-raiser? As if!"

"I don't care if you believe me. It's true!" Mickey shouted. Her eyes stung with tears. "You may all think I'm a talentless joke, but Gigi Harlowe likes—no, loves—my design." She ran out of the room to the girls' bathroom, bolted the stall door behind her, and cried. How could Mr. Kaye be so negative? Why did he always have to criticize everything she designed? Why couldn't he just appreciate her work like Gigi? And why did Jade always torment her and make her feel like a nothing?

Just then her phone dinged with a message. 4:30 Madison Plaza Hotel, Penthouse Suite A. Don't be late! Thank goodness for Gigi! Maybe they'd become BFFs. Maybe Gigi would have her over to her palatial Hamptons estate or ask her to be in her red-carpet entourage at the MTV Awards. It was all happening so fast. *Take that, FAB!*

Mickey dried her eyes and went to her next class. She'd prove to Mr. Kaye, Jade, and the rest of them that she was a great designer. When *Vogue* featured a picture of Gigi wearing her Pop Star bag, she'd show them—and they'd be very, very sorry.

6

Going Up

★ ★

"Pinch me, will ya?" JC asked Mickey as they entered the big, gold revolving doors to the lobby of the Madison Plaza Hotel.

"Pinch you? Why?" Mickey asked.

"So I know this isn't just a dream...a big, beautiful dream."

"It's real," Mickey said. "You and I are going to bring Gigi Harlowe my bag, and she is going to rock the red carpet wearing it at tonight's Pink Party fund-raiser."

"I feel a little woozy," JC said, pretending to swoon. Mickey pinched him lightly on the arm. "Ouch!" he said, rubbing it. "I was kidding!"

"No time for fainting," Mickey said, eyeing the immense lobby. Everything was adorned in gold: the banisters of the main staircase, the giant vases filled with fresh orchids, even the ceiling. "We have to figure out where the elevator is and get this to Gigi ASAP." They wandered past the marble reception desk.

A doorman dressed in a white uniform with gold epaulets on his shoulders jumped in front of them. "May I help you?"

"Yes! You can!" Mickey piped up. "We need to

get to Penthouse Suite A. We have a delivery for Gigi Harlowe."

The man looked them over and wrinkled his nose. "The penthouse floor is private and restricted. VIP guests only. No visitors allowed."

JC pushed Mickey gently aside. "You don't understand, my good man," he corrected the doorman. "We are VIPs. Gigi's expecting us. Like, now."

The man walked over to a phone at the reception desk and dialed an extension. Mickey and JC could see he was speaking to someone on the other end but couldn't make out what he was saying.

Finally, he hung up. "No visitors," he said firmly.

"What? Gigi told me to be here!" Mickey protested, showing him her text as proof.

"I spoke with her publicist, and she doesn't know about any visitors. I need to ask you to leave. Like, now."

"Look, buddy," JC said. "We're not Gigi groupies. She actually wants my friend's bag to wear to the party tonight." Mickey showed him her bubble bag.

The man sniffed. "I'm sure. The door is that way." He blew a gold whistle hanging on a chain around his neck, and two security guards began closing in on them. "This way, please."

The guards escorted JC and Mickey outside to the curb, several feet from the hotel.

"Thanks," JC snarled at them. "Appreciate the hospitality!"

Then he turned to Mickey. "Did you text Gigi? Tell her we're stuck out here and they won't let us up and her publicist is clueless?"

"I did," Mickey said with a sigh. "She's not answering. And if I don't get her that bag, she'll never speak to me again."

Suddenly, a catering truck pulled up in front of the hotel. The doorman pointed to a service entrance around the corner.

"Mick," JC said. "We're goin' in."

Mickey shook her head. "JC, they'll only bounce us out of the hotel again. Or worse: call the police."

"Not if we go through the back door." He pulled her toward the catering van. Several workers were unloading dozens of pastries and desserts. They left the door to the van wide open as they hurried inside, arms filled with trays. JC waited till no one was at the van's rear and seized the opportunity. While Mickey kept an eye on the driver, he reached in the back and grabbed two platters out—one for each of them.

"Score!" he said triumphantly and whistled through his teeth to let Mickey know to follow.

They walked through the service entrance, carefully covering their faces with the trays of éclairs and cream puffs. They strolled right past the security guard and into the service elevator.

"JC, you're amazing!" Mickey congratulated him. "How did you do that?"

"Practice," JC explained. "I've snuck backstage twice at Madonna concerts."

He hit the PH button, and the door creaked shut. "Next stop, Gigi!"

They waited patiently for the old elevator to climb eighteen stories to the very top. When they reached sixteen, it suddenly bounced and stopped. The lights flickered and went dark.

Mickey pressed the flashlight on her phone. "What just happened? What's going on?"

"Mick, don't panic," JC said, hitting the open button, then every other one on the panel.

"I won't panic if you tell me we're not stuck in here."

"Okay, then panic. Because we're stuck!" JC said.

"Ring the alarm!" Mickey shouted.

"And alert the security guard that we're trespassing? Not a good idea."

Mickey was now frantic. "Well, what do we do? Stay in here forever while Gigi goes to her fund-raiser without my bag?"

"We call in reinforcements," JC said, thinking

quickly. He checked to make sure his phone still had a signal and hit speed dial. "Madge?" he said. "We have a fashion emergency…"

It was nearly an hour before JC's eighties-loving pal managed to get uptown to the Madison Plaza with everything JC told her she needed. She was dressed in a beret and white apron, carrying a white paper bag, and quickly walked past the security guard at the service entrance with a wave of her hand. "They forgot the crème anglaise," she said in a phony French accent. "*Incroyable!* Who ever heard of serving my roasted pear and quince tarts without it?"

Madge found the service elevator and pressed the button several times, but nothing lit up or budged. JC had warned her it might not work and she would have to improvise.

"Monsieur..." She summoned the guard. "Could you perhaps alert someone to the elevator? There seems to be an issue."

The guard looked up from his newspaper. "What kind of an issue?"

"My crème is getting warm. I must get it to the Pink Party."

The man nodded and issued an order into his

walkie-talkie. "Give 'em a sec to restart it," he assured her. "It gets a little sticky sometimes."

"*Oui!* Like my sticky toffee pudding!" Madge said, walking back to his desk. "Do you like toffee? Or chocolate perhaps?" She handed him a white paper bag with a chocolate éclair inside. "For you, *mon ami*—while we're waiting."

He looked inside the bag, and his eyes lit up. "No one ever brings me a treat!"

"Well, they should," Madge said, batting her eyelashes. "They're very lucky to have you. What did you say your name was?"

"Albert," he replied. "But you can call me Al."

"Well, Al," Madge said. "Pleasure meeting

you. My name is…" She paused for a second. She hadn't really thought of a cover name! "Uh, my name is Marie Antoinette."

"That's a lovely name," Al said. "For a lovely lady."

His walkie-talkie crackled. "Elevator is up and running," a voice said on the other end.

Inside, JC and Mickey cheered as the lights came on and the elevator lurched to a start. "Yes!" JC said, fist-pumping the air. "Madge to the rescue!"

They jumped out and raced for the penthouse suite. At the door, JC suddenly froze.

"What's wrong?" Mickey asked. "Why are you just standing there like a statue?"

"I need a moment," JC said, taking a deep breath. "I'm about to meet a fashion icon. I need to process."

Mickey glanced nervously at the time on her phone. "JC, no time to process! Ring the bell!"

"Okay, okay." JC sighed. He rang, then stood with his nose pressed against the door. A hotel maid answered. "Sorry, they've all gone," she said.

"Gone?" JC gasped. "What do you mean, they've gone? Where in the name of Gaga could they have gone when they knew we were coming?"

"Gigi must have left for the party!" Mickey wailed. "What do we do now?"

JC grabbed her hand and pulled her after him.

"We take the stairs down!"

7

Party Crashers

After running down fifteen flights to the third floor, Mickey and JC raced into the grand ballroom. A woman was up at the podium giving a speech so no one was paying attention when they snuck into the room. There were dozens of tables draped in pink velvet fabric and tall floral centerpieces brimming with pink roses, begonias, and azaleas. The crystal chandeliers twinkled on the ceiling, but even more glittery were the dresses worn by all the celebrities and society elite.

"This is amazing!" Mickey said, taking it all in. "I feel like I've walked into a magical land. And it's all pink and sparkly!"

JC nodded. "I have never seen cocktail shrimp that big," he said, grabbing one from a waiter walking by. "This is impressive, all right."

They scanned the tables for Gigi, but there were too many guests to spot her.

"It's like looking for a needle in a haystack," Mickey whispered.

"Don't you mean looking for a beautiful model in a sea of beautiful people?" JC asked. "There must be over a thousand guests here!"

"You go left, I'll go right," Mickey suggested.

They split up and began making their way through the crowds and the waiters serving them dinner. JC's stomach started to growl. They had been in that elevator a really long time! He saw an open seat—and a plate of prime rib waiting at it—and sat down. Gigi could wait a few minutes longer, couldn't she?

"Pardon me," a gray-haired woman whispered to him. "I think you're in the wrong seat."

"Nuh-uh," JC replied, stuffing his mouth with potato au gratin. "I'm here."

The woman pointed to a place card that read, "M. Curtin."

"That's me," JC insisted. "Matt Curtin.

Matty to my closest friends, but Mom calls me Matthew."

"Well, Matty," the woman continued, "that must be your mother up there speaking at the podium. Madeline Curtin, chairwoman of the Pink Party?"

JC gulped. "Gee, Mommy didn't tell me she was giving a speech," he fibbed. "Good for her. Gotta go!"

He grabbed one last forkful of roast beef and ran off in search of Gigi.

Meanwhile, Mickey was having no better luck. "Excuse me." She tapped a pretty brunette on the shoulder. "Have you seen the supermodel Gigi Harlowe?"

"Nope," replied the young woman, who was wearing a pale-pink gown. "But if you do, tell her I'm mad she beat me out for the Calvin ad campaign."

Mickey looked puzzled—until she realized the woman was Kendyll Jansen, Gigi's supermodel nemesis. The two of them were always on one magazine cover or the other. Kendyll was the face of Ooh La La makeup; Gigi was the spokeswoman for NOW! nail polish. Kendyll modeled Just Sew jeans; Gigi was the official representative of Dollz Denim. They were the ultimate competitors in the supermodel world, and their feuds were legendary.

"Oh!" Mickey gasped. "Sorry!" As someone who was constantly being beaten out by Jade, she understood a little of what Kendyll was feeling.

Kendyll sighed. "Do you have any idea what it's like to have someone constantly breathing down your neck, just waiting for you to mess up or fail so she can swoop in and outdo you?"

"I do," Mickey said. "Really, I do. I go to the Fashion Academy of Brooklyn, and there's a girl there who always tries to one-up me. She makes fun of my designs, says I have no taste. It's pretty annoying."

"No kidding," Kendyll said. "I'm sick of it. It's always Gigi this, Gigi that."

"Well, for what it's worth, I loved your *Marie Claire* cover," Mickey said. "The one with the Dior print jumpsuit?"

"You did? Thanks!" Kendyll replied. "Gigi said it was lame, but I try not to listen when she moves her lips."

Mickey smiled. "That's funny. That's exactly how I handle Jade. I just tune her out and pretend it's white noise."

Kendyll smiled. "Do you have a picture of one of your designs?"

"Are you kidding? I have a whole folder on my phone!" She pulled it out and flipped through them.

"Well, I can see why Jade gives you so much trouble," Kendyll said.

"You can? Why?"

"Because you're amazingly talented! She's so jealous, she can't see straight. This army jacket with the vintage patches is sick!"

"That's probably why Gigi gives you a hard time too," Mickey said thoughtfully. "She sees you as a threat."

"Seems like we have a lot in common," Kendyll said. "What did you say your name is?"

"Mickey," she replied. "Mickey Williams."

"Well, good luck, Mickey Williams," she said. "With finding Gigi and with dealing with jealous

Jade at school. Don't let her get to you; you're better than her."

Mickey actually wanted to hug her—but she felt like Kendyll might think she was weird if she did. "You too, Kendyll," she said instead.

Mickey continued wandering around the ballroom. There were many more high-fashion models, not to mention tons of designers, movie stars, and even a presidential candidate. She wished she had time to chat with them all, but the only thing she could think about was finding Gigi and putting the purse in her hands.

"You!" a voice suddenly whispered behind her. "You were supposed to be here hours ago!"

It was Gigi—and she didn't look very happy to see her.

"I'm so sorry," Mickey told her. "We got kicked out, then stuck in the elevator. Then Madge had to spring us…"

"No excuses!" Gigi said, raising her hand. "I missed carrying the bag on the pink carpet in front of all the press."

"Oh no!" Mickey replied. "Please, take it now. I'm so sorry!"

Gigi pouted. "No. I don't want it anymore."

"Please!" Mickey pleaded. "I tried so hard to get here on time."

"Not hard enough," Gigi huffed. "Go away."

"But you loved it. Remember?" This couldn't be happening. First Mr. Kaye dissed her bag, and now Gigi!

A woman in a big fuchsia hat interrupted them from where she was sitting at a neighboring table. "Excuse me, dear," she said to Mickey. "Can I see that bag?" Mickey held it out to her, and the woman smiled. "It's quite unique. Did you make it?"

"Yes." Mickey nodded. "For my class project."

The woman beamed. "Well, I think it's wonderful."

Gigi suddenly grabbed the bag out of Mickey's hands. "It is, isn't it? I discovered it. It's mine."

"Of course!" Mickey said, relieved. "I said you can buy it."

"Buy it?" Gigi laughed in her face. "I make fashion trends. You should be paying me."

"What?" Mickey asked. "That's not fair!" She was counting on that five hundred dollars to buy a new sewing machine and a birthday present for Aunt Olive.

"You were late, so I'm not paying you a cent for it," Gigi said. "That should teach you a lesson about being punctual." She snapped her fingers, and a security guard made his way over to the table.

"We can take a hint," JC said, appearing behind Mickey. "No need to kick us to the curb again."

Then he turned to Gigi. "Can I just take a quick selfie before we go?"

"*Out!*" Gigi bellowed.

When they were outside once again, Mickey sat on the steps of the hotel and sulked.

"I know things didn't turn out the way you wanted them to," JC said, trying to comfort her. "But look on the bright side: a psycho supermodel is sporting your bag. Yippee!"

Mickey glared at him. "Really? Gigi didn't pay me. She didn't get photographed on the pink carpet carrying it. Tell me exactly, why should I be happy?"

"Okay, so maybe that bright side is a little dim…" JC said.

"It's pitch-dark. As dark as that elevator we were stuck in for over an hour," Mickey moped. "This has been the worst day of my life."

"Actually," JC reminded her, "that might be tomorrow, when you have to apologize to Mr. Kaye for mouthing off to him."

Mickey had almost forgotten about her outburst in Apparel Arts! "Oh no. He's gonna hate me."

"*Hate* is a strong word," JC said, putting an

arm around her. "Let's just say you might not be his bestie at the moment."

"I'm not Gigi's bestie either," Mickey added. "I really thought she was going to love my bag and ask me to be one of her entourage."

"You can be one of my entourage," JC offered. "As long as I don't have to pay you five hundred dollars. 'Cause I've got my eye on an original Madonna 'Holiday' single at Madge's and it's pricey."

Mickey smiled slightly. "You were amazing today, JC," she said. "What would I do without you?"

He dug in his jacket pocket and pulled out an

éclair wrapped in a napkin that he had nabbed from the pastry tray on the dinner table. "Go hungry, probably," he said, offering her half. "What are best friends for?"

8

All O-Kaye

Mickey knew she had to speak to Mr. Kaye before classes started for the day. The longer she waited, the worse it would be. But as she stood at his office door, poised to knock on it, she felt her knees knocking together as well. What if he yelled at her? What if he told her she was a terrible designer? What if he kicked her out of FAB?

The door suddenly sprang open. "I was reading my newspaper, and I thought I heard something—or someone," he said. "But then as you say, 'What do I know?'"

Mickey winced. This wasn't going to be easy. "Mr. Kaye, I want to apologize for yesterday..." she began.

"For your words, or for your project?" he asked her.

"Both, I guess."

He opened his newspaper to the gossip page and held it up for her to see. There was a photo of Gigi, wearing Mickey's Pop Star purse as she twirled around the ballroom dance floor.

"Well, it photographs well," he said.

For a brief moment Mickey was excited. Then

she remembered how mad her teacher was. "It was wrong of me to yell at you," she said. "I was just mad."

"Mad at whom?" he asked. "I believe you were mad at yourself because you know my critique was spot-on."

Mickey thought for a second. "I guess you were right about the back being slightly oval. I can kinda see that in the photo of Gigi. And I had a hard time sewing the plastic strap, so a few of my stitches were uneven…"

"My job is not to knock you down, Mickey—although I'm sure that's what you think," he explained. "It's to make you a better designer.

The only way you learn is to make mistakes and do better the next time."

Mickey nodded. "I know. It just hurt."

"The truth often hurts," Mr. Kaye added. "But you can't lie to yourself. Not if you want to be a successful designer."

"I do!" Mickey said. "I really do."

"Then let's move forward," Mr. Kaye suggested. "You will receive a two out of four on this assignment, and I hope to see a vast improvement on the next one."

Mickey hated the idea of a bad grade, but at least Mr. Kaye was leaving the door open—so to speak—for her to do better.

"I guess that's fair," she said.

"Oh, I think it's very fair," he said. "An outburst like that could have resulted in suspension from FAB."

"Thanks, Mr. Kaye. I'll do better next time."

Her teacher nodded. "I know you will. And for the future, remember that sometimes lips need to be zipped, Mackenzie, not just clothing."

The last person Mickey wanted to see after her talk with Mr. Kaye was Jade. But there she was, hovering at the end of the hall, surrounded by South and Jake.

"Mickey!" South waved to her. "Saw your bag on *Page Six* today. Awesome! It was right next to an item about my dad's new rap duet with Kanye."

Mickey tried to smile and walk past them, but Jade jumped right in front of her and stood there with her hands resting on her hips.

"You think you're the new 'It designer,' don't you?" she asked Mickey.

"What? No, I never said that, Jade."

"Well, Gigi is a personal friend of my mom's, and I know for a fact she wants nothing more to do with you."

Mickey wasn't going to argue that point. She was pretty sure Gigi would never want to speak to her again.

"Listen, Jade," she said calmly. "I don't care if I never, ever see another supermodel." She remembered what she'd told Kendyll, about how the best way to handle a hater was to ignore her and tune her out. So Mickey turned her back on Jade and checked her schedule, not even listening to the rest of her ranting.

Jade was surprised by her reaction; she was hoping Mickey would at least run to the bathroom and cry again. Frankly, it made her even angrier.

"Let it go, Jade," Jake said. "She doesn't care."

"Whatever." Jade sniffed. "Neither do I."

"Don't you believe it," South whispered to Mickey when Jade was out of earshot. "She does care. She was pea green with envy when she saw that photo of Gigi carrying your purse."

Mickey had to admit it felt good, just a little, to know that Jade was jealous of her. Even though yesterday had been disastrous, it was—as JC would call it—a bright side to an otherwise awful situation.

Mr. Kaye wasted no time in assigning his class their next major project—the spring semester final. "You're all aware that the Met Museum Costume Gala is in four weeks?" he asked his students. "It is the annual fund-raising gala to benefit the Metropolitan Museum of Art's Costume Institute. It marks the grand opening of the Costume Institute's annual fashion exhibit and follows its theme."

Jade's hand shot up. "I'm going with Mommy for the third year in a row," she said. "She's designing an amazing new gown for SJP."

"Goody for you," Mars muttered under her breath. "Name-dropper."

Mr. Kaye continued. "This year's theme is 'Black and White Ball,' based on a new exhibit of vintage black-and-white fashion photos. I want each of you to design an original evening look that would be appropriate to attend the gala."

"Like any of them would actually be going!" Jade snickered.

"Regardless, this assignment counts for forty percent of your grade," Mr. Kaye added. "So it must be flawless and FAB-worthy, and you have one week to do it. Begin sketching."

While everyone was deep in thought over their sketchbooks, Mr. Kaye called Mickey to his desk and handed her a slip of paper with a phone number on it. "Someone contacted me this morning shortly after our talk asking for the student who made the Gigi bag on *Page Six*," he said. "She said you would know her as the lady in the fuchsia hat."

Mickey vaguely remembered a woman with soft, wavy black hair asking to see her design and saying it was wonderful—right before Gigi seized it and threw her out.

"Me? Why does she want to talk to me?" Mickey asked.

"She says she is someone's aunt—Kendyll someone?"

"Kendyll Jansen? That was Kendyll's aunt?"

"Apparently," Mr. Kaye said. "She said it was urgent, so I told her I would relay the message to the student responsible."

Mickey stared down at the slip of paper.

"Are you going to stand there or call the super-model's aunt back?" he asked her. "Make haste!"

"You know who Kendyll Jansen is?" Mickey asked, amazed.

"I know a great deal more than you think," Mr. Kaye said with a wink. "I wasn't born yesterday."

"No, no, you weren't," Mickey said—then realized that might have been another insult to her teacher. "Not that you're old or anything...."

"Ms. Williams, go make your call," Mr. Kaye said. "And let me know what Mrs. Jansen has to say."

9

★ A Pretty Predicament ★

Mickey dialed the phone number and waited for Mrs. Jansen to pick up. In her mind, she went over every reason she could think of why Kendyll's aunt would want to call her. None of them were good:

1. She was angry that Mickey had spoken to her famous niece at the Pink Party. How dare she!

2. She was disgusted that Mickey gave her niece's archrival a one-of-a-kind bag. How dare she!

3. She found out that Mickey was trespassing in the hotel—and intended to report her. How dare she sneak in and pretend to be a caterer!

Mickey tried to calm herself down. She and JC had only been trying to help, and things had simply spun out of control.

"Hello?" a woman suddenly answered.

"I'm sorry! I know, 'How dare I?' I didn't mean to, honest!" Mickey quickly explained.

"I'm sure I don't know what you're talking about," the voice said. "Is this Mickey Williams? The young lady with the bubble bag at the Pink Party who spoke to my niece Kendyll?"

"Yesss," Mickey said slowly. "That's me."

"Oh, thank goodness!" the woman said. "I've been trying very hard to track you down. Kendyll recalled that you mentioned something about a fashion school in Brooklyn, so I made some inquiries and spoke to a very kind gentleman this morning who said he knew you."

"Mr. Kaye," Mickey said. "He gave me your number."

"Well, he promised he would—bless his heart! You see, Kendyll has a predicament."

"A predicament?" Mickey asked. She couldn't understand what kind of problem Kendyll Jansen could possibly have. She was rich and famous and one of the biggest supermodels in the world—all at the age of seventeen! "I'm not sure I know what you mean, or how I could help."

"You're a designer, are you not?" Mrs. Jansen inquired. "She said you showed her your designs and they were wonderful."

"Um, yes. I'm a designer, kinda. I'm training to be a designer at FAB, but sometimes, well, my designs don't go over very well."

"Really?" Kendyll's aunt continued. "Because that lovely gentleman told me you are one of his star pupils with one of the brightest futures in fashion."

"He said that? About me?" Mickey couldn't

believe her ears. Did Mr. Kaye actually sing her praises?

"He did. And he told me you were the perfect person for the job."

"The job? What job?" Mickey's heart was racing.

"I want you to design my niece a one-of-a-kind gown to wear to the Met Costume Gala."

Mickey held the phone away from her ear and shook it. She must have heard wrong! "Lemme get this straight. You want me to make Kendyll Jansen a dress?"

"Not just a dress—a showstopper that takes people's breath away. Something that turns heads and makes Gigi Harlowe green with envy. I was very impressed with your bag, and Kendyll mentioned that she really connected with you. She's tired of all the other designers throwing clothes at her. She wants someone fresh, young, and new that will wow the fashion world. And that would be you."

Mickey couldn't speak. She was still trying to process what Mrs. Jansen was saying.

"Dear? Did you hear me? Are you still there?" she asked Mickey.

"I'm here," Mickey said. "I'm just in shock."

"Can we make a time for you to come meet with Kendyll, take her measurements, maybe present her some ideas? The Met Gala is only a month away."

Mickey nodded, then realized Mrs. Jansen couldn't see her through the phone. "Yes, I can do that."

"Say tomorrow?"

Tomorrow! Mickey was supposed to come up with a showstopping gown idea by tomorrow? She wanted to scream, "No way!" but instead, she answered, "No prob." This was too big an opportunity to pass up. She had messed up her chance with one supermodel; she wasn't going to mess this up too.

"There's just one little thing," Mrs. Jansen added. Of course! There had to be a catch! "It has to be top secret. You can't tell anyone you're working on Kendyll's dress until after she wears it to the gala, and you can't show the final dress to anyone."

"But Mr. Kaye has to grade me on it," Mickey pointed out. "And he's really good at keeping secrets. Oh! And my best friend, JC, and my aunt Olive and my mom…"

"No one," Mrs. Jansen insisted. "Tell your teacher you are working on something for Kendyll, but don't be specific. And I'm sorry, but you'll need to make another dress for your homework. We can't risk it being leaked. As for the rest of your friends and family, you can't say anything to them either."

Mickey remembered the advice Mr. Kaye had given her in his office: "Sometimes lips need to be zipped, not just clothing."

She took a deep breath. "You've got yourself a deal," she said. "One 'wow' gown coming up!" But she knew she really had to design two wow ones—Kendyll's and another that would equally impress Mr. Kaye and keep her fellow classmates from asking questions.

Granny Gertie

Mickey hated keeping secrets—especially from her mom. But when Jordana called that night to ask her daughter how her day went, Mickey crossed her fingers behind her back and fibbed. She had promised Mrs. Jansen she wouldn't spill just yet. So she told herself it wasn't really a lie; it was just pushing the pause button on the truth.

"My day? Oh, it was fine, nothing out of the

ordinary," she told her mom. "Mr. Kaye gave us our new project to work on."

"And what's that?" her mother asked.

"It's based on the Met Costume Gala. I have to come up with something someone would wear to it." She paused. "Of course, no one would really wear one of my designs."

"Aw, don't put yourself down, Mickey Mouse!" her mom said. "Any of those big celebs would be lucky to wear a Mickey Williams original!"

"But they wouldn't. Trust me. Not happening."

"Well, then it's their loss," her mom added. "So what are you thinking of making?"

Mickey closed her eyes and brainstormed out loud. "Well, the exhibit is based on old black-and-white photographs. So I thought of creating an original textile print out of old pics."

"Sounds promising," her mom replied.

"We have this amazing scanner and fabric printer at FAB. I just have to find the right photos to use for it."

"Check with your aunt Olive," Jordana said. "She has boxes and boxes of old family photos stored away."

Mickey's ears perked up. "Really? What kind of photos?"

"Oh, lots and lots of your great-grandma Gertie

in particular. Did you know she was a silent-screen actress?"

Mickey shook her head. "No, I didn't."

"Apparently, a director spotted her and used her as an extra in a 1920s Gloria Swanson movie. Granny Gertie loved to tell us that story when we were little, all about how she was famous for fifteen minutes on the big screen. Olive just adored her."

"I think I know what I'm going to do for my design," Mickey said, inspired. "Mom, you're a genius."

"Really? What?" her mom asked excitedly. "Tell me!"

Mickey hesitated. "I can't. A designer is supposed to keep her work close to the vest—so to speak." Mickey knew her mom wasn't going to accept that answer. It was not like her to keep secrets between them.

"Since when?" Jordana asked suspiciously. "You usually text me pics of your sketches and can't wait to tell me what you're working on."

"I know, but this is different. I kind of promised I wouldn't share it. Not just yet."

"Hmm," her mom replied. "Okay, but when you are ready to share, I'll be here…waiting."

"I know," Mickey said. She felt just awful! Why had she made this stupid promise to Mrs. Jansen?

"Good luck with your top secret assignment," Jordana added. "But it's no secret that I love you, Mickey Mouse."

Mickey opened her mouth. She wanted to tell her mom so badly that she was designing a gown for Kendyll and this could finally put her name on the fashion map! But instead she replied simply, "Ditto."

After she hung up with her mom, Mickey went in search of Olive, who was hard at work in the kitchen preparing dinner.

"What is that?" Mickey asked, smelling something strange cooking in a pot on the stove.

"Alfalfa stew," Olive announced proudly. "My famous recipe."

Mickey pulled up a stool and watched her stir. "Speaking of famous…" she began. "Do you have any old black-and-white photos of Granny Gertie?"

Olive stopped what she was doing and looked thoughtful. "Oh, I haven't heard that name in ages. Dear, dear Granny Gertie! Where did you hear it?"

"Mom," Mickey explained. "She said you have a whole box of pics, and I need them for my Apparel Arts project."

Olive wiped her hands on her apron and left the stew simmering. "Follow me."

She pulled out a step stool and climbed high in the coat closet in the living room. From the top shelf, she pulled down a large shoe box.

"This should be it," she said to Mickey. "I always thought one day I'd organize them into an album or a scrapbook, a tribute to my grandma."

Mickey opened the lid and dove in. There were literally dozens of black-and-white photos of a beautiful brunette with big, dark eyes, in all sorts of fashionable attire. "I love this one," she said, finding a picture of Gertie in a flapper dress with her hair in a boyish bob. "She's so chic!"

"The chic-est." Olive smiled. "You see those long pearls? She gave those to me. I still have them."

"Aunt Olive, these are perfect," Mickey said. "Can I borrow them for a while?"

"Of course! Gertie would have loved her great-granddaughter taking an interest in her."

Mickey felt more than interested; she felt inspired, like someone had literally sparked a match and lit her creativity on fire! She could see Kendyll's gown as plain as day: a 1920s-style evening gown with an asymmetrical handkerchief hemline, a plunging V in the back, and a white marabou feather wrap. She took the shoe box and retreated to her room where she sketched and sketched until Aunt Olive called her to dinner. When she met Kendyll tomorrow, Mickey would have so much to show her!

The next day felt like it was dragging on forever. Mickey just wanted it to end so she could get to Mrs. Jansen's apartment on the Upper East Side.

"Hey, Mick." JC waved at her as she bounded down the front steps of FAB in search of her school bus. "Where ya goin' in such a hurry?"

She checked the time on her phone: 3:15 p.m. She had promised Mrs. Jansen she would be there no later than four thirty to meet with her and Kendyll. If JC slowed her down, or worse, if she missed her bus, she'd be late.

"Can't talk now." She hurried past him. "Call ya later."

"But what about Madge? You said you would come with me after school and help me pick out some albums."

Mickey froze in her tracks. She had promised JC she would go with him. It had completely flown out of her head when this whole Kendyll costume popped up.

"I'm sorry, JC," she apologized. "I just can't today. I'm in a huge rush."

"Okay," JC said. "Where ya rushin' to? Maybe I can come, and we can go to Madge another day."

"No!" Mickey shouted, a little louder than she intended. "You can't come with me."

"Why not?" JC asked. He sniffed his armpit, then Madonna's bag. "Neither one of us smells."

"I can't say," Mickey said, lowering her eyes. "It's kind of a secret."

"Since when do we keep secrets from each other?" Mickey noticed that JC looked genuinely upset. But she couldn't tell him; she just couldn't!

"We don't. But this is a super secret, and I just can't share it with anyone," she tried to explain.

"I'm not just anyone. I'm your best friend."

Mickey nodded. "You are! And I promise, as soon as I can say something, I will."

She patted his arm and dashed off just as the school bus was getting ready to pull away. Keeping this secret was going to be harder than she'd thought—especially if it meant hurting JC's feelings in the process.

Model Meeting

"Mickey!" Kendyll said as she opened the door to her aunt's fancy Park Avenue apartment. "I'm so glad you're here!"

Mickey smiled shyly. "You are?"

"Are you kidding?" Kendyll said, motioning for her to come in. "I think you're the perfect person to design my gala gown. I'm so excited to see what you're thinking."

"Let her take her coat off first," Mrs. Jansen

said, chuckling. "As you can tell, Kendyll is a little excited."

"A little? I'm so psyched!" her niece said. "No one is going to have a gown like this."

"Especially not Gigi," Mickey reminded her with a wink.

"May I offer you some tea?" Mrs. Jansen asked, bringing in a silver platter stacked with mini sandwiches.

"Don't mind if I do," Mickey said, helping herself to a tiny triangle filled with ham and cheese. "My aunt is a vegetarian, so her idea of a yummy after-school snack is a tofu fritter."

Kendyll wrinkled her nose. "Eww, gross! Do you live with your aunt?"

"I do," Mickey said. "So I can attend FAB in New York. My mom is back home in Philly."

"We really are a lot alike," Kendyll added. "I live with my aunt Elinore while my mom and dad live in Boca. So I can shoot magazine covers and ads and stuff here in the city."

"I don't make you eat tofu fritters," Mrs. Jansen pointed out.

"No, but you do make me eat those weird little broccoli pies sometimes for breakfast!"

"They're called quiche," her aunt remarked. "I make delicious broccoli-and-cheddar quiche for brunch."

Kendyll shook her head no, and Mickey

giggled. After she had stuffed her face with sand-wiches and scones, she took a pile of sketches out of her bag. They showed the black-and-white photo dress from every angle.

Neither Kendyll nor Mrs. Jansen said any-thing. Mickey looked from face to face, trying to figure out what they might be thinking. Did they hate it? Was it all wrong? She cleared her throat and nervously twirled her hair around her finger.

"Divine," Mrs. Jansen finally proclaimed. "You were right, Kendyll. She's quite a talent."

Mickey breathed a huge sigh of relief. "I want to use these photos for the print," she said, pulling a stack of Granny Gertie's pics out and laying them across the coffee table.

"She's beautiful! Who is she?" Kendyll gasped.

"My great-grandma."

Mrs. Jansen took out her checkbook. "So we're all agreed then. You'll make this dress for Kendyll, and we will cover all the expenses and however many hours you put into it. Will this be enough to start you off?"

She ripped out the check and handed it to Mickey. It read, "Pay to the order of Mickey Williams: Five hundred dollars."

"I can't," Mickey said. "I can't take all this

money. It won't cost nearly that much because I'll make the fabric print myself."

She thought about how excited she had been when Gigi offered to pay her that for her purse. But now it felt selfish.

"Mickey, a big fashion designer gets a lot of money to make a gala gown," Kendyll tried to explain. "Thousands and thousands."

"I know, but I'm not a big designer yet. And you're giving me a chance to be one. Let me make the dress, and if you like it, we'll figure out a way for you to pay me back. For now, all I need is about fifty dollars to buy the silk I need for printing. I found some great marabou in the FAB scrap bin and the most amazing, delicate lace trim for the neckline."

"Waste not, want not," Mrs. Jansen said, writing Mickey another check for fifty dollars.

"Yes, ma'am," Mickey said. "My mom showed me how to shop for flea-market finds, and my aunt Olive never wastes anything. She's a whiz at whipping up a whole week's worth of dinners out of leftovers."

"Sounds like someone could learn something from you," Mrs. Jansen said, patting Kendyll on the knee. "Kendyll is a shopaholic."

"I can't help it." She shrugged. "Fashion is my passion."

"Mine too," Mickey said. "I can show you some really cool ways to recycle old clothes into whole new outfits. See this skirt?" She pointed to the red plaid mini she had chosen to wear this morning. "I made it out of an old lumberjack shirt I got at the thrift store for six dollars. I thought the black fringe on the bottom would make it a little edgier."

"I love it. It looks like something off the runway," Kendyll marveled. "You create magic, Mickey. You're like a fashion fairy god-friend or something!"

Mickey laughed. "Wow, no one has ever called me a fairy god-friend! I'll take it as a compliment."

"You should," Mrs. Jansen said. "We're very impressed and very excited to see the dress come to life. When do you suppose you can come back for Kendyll's first fitting?"

Mickey tapped her pencil on her chin. "Well, let's see... I was supposed to go home to Philly this weekend, and I promised JC I'd hang with him Sunday night. But I could cancel both. This is more important..."

Kendyll hugged Mickey. "I can't thank you enough," she said. "And I can't wait to tell everyone who asks me at the gala, 'Who are you wearing?' that I'm in an original design by Mickey Williams!"

"Wait, you're standing me up again?" JC groaned. "Mickey, this is the second time in a week!"

"JC, I'm really sorry," Mickey apologized. "But I have this huge project I need to get done." What she really wanted to tell him was, "I have two huge projects: one for Apparel Arts, one for Kendyll Jansen!"

"The Met Gala thing?" JC asked.

Mickey gasped. "What? Huh?" Had she let something slip?

"Mr. Kaye's assignment—isn't that what you're working on?"

"Oh, yeah!" Mickey said, covering. "Yes. That's it. I have to get my gala dress all finished to present in class on Monday, and I haven't even started."

"You said you've been working on it nonstop," JC reminded her. "Remember?"

Mickey tried to think fast. "Well, I scrapped the old idea. Now I'm doing a whole new one. I'm trying to impress Mr. Kaye. You know, because I got in trouble and all?"

"Uh-huh."

Mickey had a feeling JC wasn't buying her story, but there was nothing she could do about it. She needed the weekend to work on the dress for Kendyll, and she needed to come up with a design for Mr. Kaye.

"Fine." JC sniffed. "Do what you have to do. Madonna and I will muddle through without you."

Her mom was equally annoyed. "Mickey, that's three weekends in a row you haven't come home," she complained. "I've forgotten what you look like."

"I'll send you a selfie. The blue highlights in my hair are awesome," Mickey teased. "I promise I'll take the train home next weekend."

"That's what you said last week…and the week before that," her mom said. "I think you're working too hard."

"But that's a good thing, isn't it?" Mickey tried

to convince her. "You want me to do well in my classes, right?"

"Of course I do," her mom said, relenting. "But I miss you, Mickey Mouse."

"I miss you too, Mom. But you're going to be really proud when you see what I'm making.'"

Her mom smiled. "I'm always proud of you, peanut," she said. "I just feel like you're keeping something from me."

Mickey gulped. How did her mom guess? "Don't be silly!" she said, pretending to laugh. "What would I be keeping from you?"

"I dunno," Jordana answered. "But I know my kid. Something is up."

Mickey hung up and hoped she had put her mom's concerns to rest. All she had to do was get through the next three weeks before the gala. Then everything would be revealed, and her mom and JC would understand and applaud her. She hoped…

★ Not So Black and White ★

Mickey spent all weekend stitching together Kendyll's gown from the fabric she had printed at FAB. She loved how the photos of Gertie seemed to leap off the silk. From a distance, it was a striking black-and-white pattern; but up close, the tintype photos were vibrant and dramatic and had a silent-movie feel.

"Planning on coming up for air?" Olive asked, poking her head into Mickey's bedroom and sewing studio.

"Not just yet," Mickey said, focusing on the

stitches needed to hem each handkerchief layer. "My machine is giving me trouble again, so I need to do this all by hand."

Olive tried to sneak a peek, but Mickey grabbed the dress and hid it under her sewing table. "It's not ready to be seen," she said.

"I'm sure it's perfect," Olive said. "But I think it could use one little thing." She pulled out a velvet box and handed it to her. "I found this and thought you should have it."

Mickey gently eased the box open. "The pearls! Gertie's pearls!"

"I thought it would be the perfect accessory," Olive said, smiling.

Mickey hugged her. "It is. You sure you don't mind?"

"Mind?" Olive replied. "They've been sitting in my drawer for years. They need to get an airing." Mickey knew Kendyll would simply flip out when she showed her the vintage necklace. The string was a bit frayed but seemed strong enough.

"So your project's due Monday?" Olive asked.

Mickey was suddenly seized by panic. She had been spending so much time on Kendyll's dress that she'd barely given her Apparel Arts assignment a second thought. Monday was only two days away!

"I guess it is," she told her aunt. "I'm gonna be working day and night to get it done."

Olive nodded. "Then you'll need my famous kale cookies to keep you awake," she said. "I'll go bake up a batch. Maybe two."

Mickey looked at her sketchbook. She had quickly come up with a masquerade-themed dress using black-and-white diamond patches fitted together to resemble a jester's costume. Compared to Kendyll's dress, it felt silly. But she had no choice; she had to show Mr. Kaye something— anything but the real gala gown she was making. She began cutting triangles out of scraps of fabric and stitching them together, hoping something magical would take place and her laughable dress would be transformed into an A+ outfit.

But all she could think about were two little words that Jade loved to throw in her face: "As if!"

Apparel Arts was first period Monday, and Mickey had a finished dress to show Mr. Kaye. Even if it wasn't perfect, at least it wouldn't be another incomplete.

"You have to see mine," Gabriel said, pulling a jumpsuit out of his garment bag and setting it on his dress form. "I was inspired by chess pieces." She noticed that he had made his own textile as well, silk-screened with images of black and white bishops, queens, kings, and knights. The hat that went with it had a giant cross on top, like a king piece.

"It's amazing," Mickey said, feeling the soft, silky fabric. "Mr. Kaye is gonna love it."

Mars's look was equally stunning: a black wire-mesh skirt over an off-white velvet catsuit. She had paired it with an enormous medallion necklace fashioned from the bottom of a soda can. "I made the jewelry myself," she said. "I wanted it to feel like industrial meets feminine."

Jade and Jake had teamed up on theirs: complementing black-and-white tuxedo looks. Jake's was a black pantsuit with wide-legged trousers, while Jade's was a white strapless gown with a chiffon balloon skirt underneath a tiny, cropped black satin jacket. Even Mickey had to admit, both outfits were breathtaking.

South had gone with black hip-hop-inspired harem pants and a white off-the-shoulder cashmere sweater. Around the neckline and cuffs, she had hand-stitched tiny seed pearls. "Wow," Mickey said. "The detail is amazing."

South smiled. "I'm really proud of it. I think it's my best work yet. Lemme see yours."

Mickey pulled her dress out of its bag. The skirt was made of jagged, diamond-shaped satin patches, and the collar curled high around the back of the neck. South looked at it, confused. "It's, it's…interesting," she said. "Maybe a little too literal? It feels like a costume for a costume party. Or maybe a clown dress?"

Mickey winced. "Is it that bad?"

South wrinkled her nose. "Kinda. It just doesn't feel like you, Mickey."

Mr. Kaye came in, glanced at Mickey's dress displayed on its form, and raised an eyebrow.

"Mackenzie, this is yours?" he asked.

Mickey shrugged. "Um, yeah. I guess it is."

"This is your dress for the Met Gala Ball?" her teacher repeated.

Mickey nodded. "Seems like it." If only she had spent more time thinking it through! Or if only she could show Mr. Kaye what she had really been working on. He would love the Kendyll gown so much more.

He scribbled some notes in his grading book, then continued making his way around the room, checking everyone's work. When the bell rang for the next period, Mr. Kaye pointed directly at Mickey and motioned for her to come speak to him at his desk.

"Are you telling me that this is what you are putting on Kendyll Jansen to wear to the Met Gala?" he asked her when everyone else had left the room. "Good heavens! Are you trying to humiliate us both?"

Mickey looked shocked. "What? You know about Kendyll?"

"I surmised. I didn't think Mrs. Jansen would call me in such a panic unless there was a gala gown at stake."

"You can't tell anyone," Mickey begged him. "I promised. No one can know."

"I assume this is not the actual dress," he continued. "I hope and pray it isn't."

Mickey pulled the real gown out of her garment bag, the one she was taking to Kendyll for a fitting this afternoon.

Mr. Kaye examined it closely. "The stitches are flawless," he said. "All hand done?"

"I had no choice," Mickey said. "My sewing machine is on its last legs."

"And the textile is breathtaking—you made it as well?"

"See this?" she said, pointing to a photo of a woman in a flapper dress and fur jacket. "That's my granny Gertie on the set of a Gloria Swanson movie."

"Clever. Resourceful. Authentic," Mr. Kaye muttered under his breath.

"Is that good?" Mickey asked hopefully.

"It's your best work yet," he said. "It shows

an expert hand, a critical eye, and a luminous imagination."

"Can I have it back?" Mickey asked softly. "I kinda have to fit it to Kendyll today."

"Not yet," Mr. Kaye insisted. He took a slip of paper out of his desk drawer, scribbled something on it, and folded it in half. "Now you may."

Mickey zipped the gown back in its bag just as Mr. Kaye handed her the paper. "Open it," he said. "It deserves review."

Mickey closed her eyes and unfolded the note. *Please*, she silently prayed, *let it be better than a 2!* On it was 4+ written in bright-red pen.

"My first 4+ of the semester," he told her. "Extremely well-deserved."

Mickey beamed. *He liked it! He really, really liked it!* "Thank you," she said simply.

"Don't thank me," Mr. Kaye told her. "You did this all on your own. I predict Mrs. Jansen will be very pleased. Do send my regards."

"Um, could I maybe not?" Mickey asked. "Just 'cause it's supposed to be a secret?"

Mr. Kaye pretended to zip his lips shut. "And I predict great things ahead for you, Mackenzie. As long as you continue to do this kind of work and believe in yourself."

Fit and Fabulous

Kendyll came out of her aunt's dressing room and twirled around. The handkerchief layers swirled around her and settled gently around her ankles. Mickey couldn't believe her eyes: the gown fit her like a glove.

"I don't know what to say," Kendyll said, looking at herself in a full-length mirror.

"Say you like it," Mickey replied, crossing her fingers. "Say it's okay?"

"Okay? It's gorgeous!" Kendyll replied. "I've never seen anything so beautiful."

Mrs. Jansen nodded and dabbed her eyes with a tissue. "It makes me teary," she said. "Exquisite. Simply exquisite."

Mickey fussed a bit over the V in the back. "Maybe I'll bring this up a half inch," she said. Then she checked the fit around the waist and hips. "And maybe taper this just a tad?"

"Mickey, I can't thank you enough," Kendyll added. "It's everything I dreamed my first Met Gala gown would be and more."

"Oh! I almost forgot!" Mickey took the velvet necklace box out of her bag. "These were Gertie's.

My aunt Olive let me borrow them. You can wear them—if you want."

Kendyll took the delicate pearls in her hands. "Oh my gosh. Are these vintage? From the twenties?"

"Yeah, I know. They're a little beat up. You prob don't want to wear them…"

"I do!" Kendyll said, cradling them in her palms. "May I? They're so special."

"Sure," Mickey said. "Maybe a little silver polish would fix up the tarnish on the clasp?"

Mrs. Jansen took the pearls from her niece. "Don't you worry," she assured both of them. "I'll take care of it."

Kendyll continued marveling at the dress in the mirror. "How did you do the antique lace ticking around the neckline?" she asked. "It's so precisely placed."

"All by hand," Mickey said. "It actually turned out to be a good thing that my sewing machine is about to die."

When Kendyll had taken the dress off, Mickey packed it up to take home and make a few more adjustments.

"I can bring it back to you this Thursday," she told the Jansens. "No prob." That actually left her the weekend to go home to Philly and Friday afternoon to make up with JC.

"Perfect," Mrs. Jansen remarked. "And then it's only two more weeks till you can tell the world our little secret. I know it must be very hard for you to keep it from your family and classmates."

"It is," Mickey admitted. "But it'll be totally worth it when Kendyll rocks my design on the red carpet."

"Totally," Kendyll repeated. "I can't wait."

JC was thrilled to spend an afternoon combing the East Village with Mickey in search of old eighties albums and some cool fashion finds.

"Is it me?" he asked, modeling a navy suit jacket with huge shoulder pads he found on a rack in a vintage shop.

"Um, not so much." Mickey chuckled. She pulled out another option—a purple-and-black-checked blazer—and handed it to him.

"You know me so well," he said. "I'll take it."

They were strolling the streets of the village, munching on cronuts from the Dominique Ansel Bakery, when JC suddenly stopped. "Okay, you need to tell me what's been going on with you," he said. "I know you're keeping something from me."

He sounded just like her mom! "You have to

trust me, JC," Mickey said. "I'll tell you as soon as I can."

"Is it good…or deep, dark, and awful?" he asked, concerned.

"Is what awful?" Mickey asked.

"The secret. Kaye isn't kicking you out of FAB, is he?"

"What? No! No way!" Mickey laughed. "I'm not going anywhere."

"You sure? You haven't decided to pack up and leave Oz for Kansas, Dorothy?"

Mickey rolled her eyes. "As if! Would I ever leave FAB and my BFF?"

JC took a bite of his cream-filled pastry. "Okay.

Just checkin'. You were making me nervous there." Madonna barked from inside her bag. "Madonna too. She's gotten really used to you."

Mickey linked arms with JC. "Well, thanks, Madonna," she said. "I've gotten used to you too. Both of you."

The Big Reveal

The two weeks till the gala seemed to fly by. Before Mickey knew it, she was sitting in Mrs. Jansen's apartment for the last time, helping Kendyll get into her gown while her stylists fussed with her hair and makeup. She'd chosen to wear her hair in a faux bob, with her waves carefully tucked under to resemble Gertie's in the photos.

She added white satin elbow-length gloves,

sky-high silver sandals, and a black sequin mask to accessorize the dress.

"One more thing," her aunt said, racing around to get herself ready in time as well. "This is for both of you. For Kendyll to wear tonight, and for Mickey to have as a memento after the gala." She brought out a Tiffany blue box, and Kendyll untied the bow. Inside were Gertie's pearls, meticulously restrung and fastened with a brilliant diamond clasp.

"Auntie Elinore! I can't believe you did this!" Kendyll gushed.

"Me, neither," Mickey said, shaking her head. "It's too, too much. I can't accept it."

"Oh, you can and you will—as payment for making this divine dress," Mrs. Jansen insisted. "And this as well." She snapped her fingers, and one of Kendyll's assistants appeared carrying a Singer sewing machine with a big red bow on top. "Top of the line, brand-new model," she said proudly. "It has all the bells and whistles. So when we hire you to make more of Kendyll's clothes, you have the very best machine to use."

Mickey wanted to cry. It was too good to be true! And the necklace would be the perfect sentimental birthday gift for Aunt Olive!

"I wish you could come with me to the gala," Kendyll said, taking Mickey's hand. "So when

Gigi comes up and says something obnoxious, you're there to help me think of a zinger to hurl back at her."

"You don't need me," Mickey assured her. "Just believe in yourself. And you've got Gertie along to help you." She pointed to a photo on the bodice of the dress. "This is my favorite one. She's doing the Charleston and kicking her leg way up in the air. If Gigi acts up, give her a kick in the butt just like that."

Kendyll cracked up. "Okay, I will."

Her stylists checked her red lipstick one last time to make sure it was set. "Do I look okay?" she asked Mickey. "I'm so, so nervous."

"You look amazing," Mickey said, hugging her. "Like the star you are."

Mickey watched as a long, black stretch limo pulled away from the Park Avenue town house and took the Jansens to the gala. It wasn't quite Cinderella's carriage, but it felt like it. And she felt a little like Kendyll's fashion fairy god-friend.

"Brava," said a voice in the shadows. Mickey recognized it at once.

"JC! What are you doing here?" she asked, shocked.

"Followed ya after school," he said. "The dress is amazing, Mick. Really. You outdid yourself."

"You know?"

"Well, now I do," he said, patting himself on the back. "Thanks to my expert spy skills."

"I know—lots of practice sneaking backstage at Madonna concerts," Mickey said, laughing.

"Exactly. You didn't think you could pull one over on me, did you?"

"Are you mad I didn't tell you? I promised Kendyll I wouldn't. Not till after the gala."

"Mad? No. Not when I know my BFF is going to make sure I get a selfie with my fave super-model next time she sees her."

"I thought Gigi was your fave supermodel," Mickey reminded him.

"Are you kidding? After the way she treated you? She's on my Who's Out list from now on."

Mickey gathered up her new sewing machine. "Look what I got as a thank-you present," she said.

JC's eyes lit up. "Okay, that is one sick sewing machine. And you will let your BFF use it, of course."

"Of course!" Mickey said, walking to the corner to hail a cab. "You coming? I hear they're streaming the Met Costume Gala live on Style.com."

"Wouldn't miss it for the world," JC said. "There's this new designer making her debut on the red carpet: Mickey Williams."

"She's supposed to be pretty good," Mickey teased.

A cab pulled up, and JC opened the door for her. "Yeah, not too shabby," he joked. "Not too shabby at all."

As she had promised, Kendyll credited Mickey with her magnificent Met Gala gown, and when *Style Snoop* magazine ran their Best Dressed of the week, there was her name, right in the caption: "Kendyll Jansen turned heads in an original Mickey Williams creation..." Mickey clipped the picture out and tucked it into the box with Granny Gertie's old photos for safekeeping. Then she texted a photo of the dress to her mom.

"I hated having to keep it from you," she said. "I almost even spilled a couple of times."

"I knew," her mom said.

"You knew? What do you mean? How?"

"I didn't know specifically, but I felt in my bones that you were working on something more than just your school assignment. Moms always know."

Mickey wondered if the rest of her FAB classmates had figured it out as well. At any rate, the cat was now out of the bag. There had been a lot of press about her gown. *Entertainment Tonight* called Kendyll "a walking work of art" and *People* magazine dubbed it "a dynamic gala debut."

"Congrats!" South said as Mickey took her seat. "You're, like, famous!"

Jade looked up but didn't say anything—not that Mickey thought she ever would. Her mom's gala gown for Gigi had gotten only mediocre reviews. One critic said the black-and-white tulle made the supermodel look like "the Goodyear blimp." But Jake warmly patted Mickey on the back. "Nice job," he said. "I bet lots of celebrities are gonna want you to design for them now."

Mickey hadn't even thought of that possibility! Jade groaned—clearly, she had.

"As if," she said through gritted teeth. "You know all those eighties pop stars who were one-hit wonders?" she asked Mickey. "That's you in the fashion world. You got lucky this one and only time."

Gabriel sprung to her defense. "Luck had nothing to do with it," he said. "Mickey is talented. And you're jealous, Jade."

"Jealous? Why should I be jealous? I've clearly got a long and successful career in fashion ahead of me."

"Yeah," Mars replied, snickering. "When your mommy retires, she'll hand you the business on a silver platter. Tell her, Mickey!"

But Mickey didn't feel the need to say anything. Jade's insults just rolled right off her, like she was wearing a big, yellow rain slicker. She remembered what she had told Kendyll that first time they met in the Madison Plaza ballroom: When it comes to haters hating on you, tune it out.

"You should be really proud of yourself, Mickey," South added. "You done good, girl."

Mickey smiled. She had done good. Not just good, great.

Jade was about to fire off another catty response when Mr. Kaye walked into the studio. He had surely seen Mickey's name in the fashion reports, but he didn't mention it. It was just like him to keep things business as usual—and keep Mickey on her toes.

"Our next assignment is going to be your toughest one yet," he warned his students. "I want you to challenge yourselves more than you ever have."

Mickey smiled. She wouldn't have it any other way.

Carrie's Style File

Meet Nancy Vuu, Kids' Couture Designer

I have had the huge honor of walking not once, but twice, in Nancy Vuu's runway show during New York Fashion Week! I love her clothes because they feel "princessy" in a very grown-up way. She creates incredible gowns and dresses in gorgeous patterns and lush fabrics—like nothing I had ever seen before. *Vogue* says she is "taking the children's fashion industry by storm" and her collections have appeared in *Harper's Bazaar* and *Elle*. She often accessorizes her runway looks with angel wings or a crown. What could be more special? Every time I get my first look at her new line, it takes my breath away. I asked Nancy if she would tell me all about her style and her inspiration.

Carrie: Did you always know you would be a fashion designer?

Nancy: As a little girl I loved to sketch fashion, and my dream was to become a fashion designer. But life took over and those dreams were long buried. Fast forward almost twenty-five years when I had a divine encounter which changed the course of my life and ushered me into my destiny.

Carrie: How would you describe Nancy Vuu Couture? What inspires you? Do you sketch your designs?

Nancy: Nancy Vuu is a luxury couture brand that styles the entire family with a focus on children and teens. My biggest inspiration is my faith. Our vision is to remind every child and teen out there that no matter their circumstance, they are wonderfully made and of true royalty. And yes I do and still love to sketch!

Carrie: Where are some of the most amazing places you have done a runway show?

Nancy: Cannes Fashion Festival, the UK, New York Fashion Week, and LA Fashion Week to name a few. Our fashion has also walked and made repeated appearances on the world-famous red carpet at the Cannes Film Festival in 2015 and 2016.

Carrie: What advice do you have for kids who want to grow up one day and be designers?

Nancy: Dream big. Work smart. Stay focused. And never let anyone dull your sparkle!

Me with Nancy Vuu at New York Fashion Week, September 2015

Walking the runway in Nancy's design

Acknowledgments

Many thanks to our friends and family for their love and support! We couldn't do this without you.

A big shout-out to Nancy Vuu for giving Carrie the opportunity to walk the runway in New York Fashion Week in her stunning couture designs! And to Sally Miller, her ultimate dress designer, for always outfitting her in the fabbest of fashions. And to East Coast Starz/ECUSA Pageants' Stacie

Weil-Fitzgerald, Elizabeth Percy, and Lauren Handler; Amaryllis Rodriguez/Showstoppers. You all gave Carrie such confidence and taught her how to strut the runway with style. We love you always!

Thanks to the crew at Sourcebooks (Steve, Kate, Elizabeth) and our gang at Folio Lit (Katherine, Frank).

DON'T MISS MICKEY'S NEXT

FABULOUS FASHION ADVENTURE!

Fashion
Face-Off

About the Authors

Sheryl Berk has written about fashion for more than twenty years, first as a contributor to *InStyle* magazine and later as the founding editor in chief of *Life & Style Weekly*. She has written dozens of books with celebrities, including Britney Spears, Jenna Ushkowitz, Whitney Port, and Zendaya— and the #1 *New York Times* bestseller (turned movie) *Soul Surfer* with Bethany Hamilton. Her daughter, Carrie Berk, is a renowned cupcake connoisseur and blogger (facebook.com/ PLCCupcakeClub; carriescupcakecritique.shutterfly.com) with more than 100,000 followers at the age of thirteen! Carrie is a fountain of fabulous ideas for book series—she came up with Fashion Academy in the fifth grade. Carrie learned to sew from her grandma "Gaga" and has outfitted many an American Girl doll in original fashions. The Berks also write the deliciously popular series The Cupcake Club.

Check out Carrie's new fashion blog: fashionacademybook.com.